Railed

A Why Cho-Cho-Choose Romance

Zane E. Stori

Railed: A Why Cho-Cho-Choose Romance

Published by The Library of Sarah Zane

Ebook ISBN: 979-8-9953203-0-2

Paperback: 979-8-9953203-1-9

Cover Design: Zane E Stori

Formatting: Zane E Stori

Editing: Kendra Wilson – Curious Minds Editing

To HR, LR, and RE for encouraging the chaos
I know you didn't think I would actually do it,
but I committed to the bit,
so now you all have first class tickets to the crazy train...
All board

Chapter One

Emma

I laid my head back on the headrest and let the gentle back and forth of the train car soothe me. After a long day at work, there was nothing more relaxing than the loving caress of the railway. It was just what I needed today.

The Save the Railways project I'd been spearheading wasn't going as I'd hoped. Train ticket sales were down, and car traffic was up on the island. My boss was supportive, but couldn't hide her concern that the project was doomed and that I was wasting my efforts.

I couldn't really blame her; the trains were only tangentially part of my job. As the head of tourism marketing, I should have been focusing on other things, like the upcoming festivals. The trains were a passion project of mine, though, and with the new car company petitioning to shut down the railways, I couldn't let it go.

Unfortunately, my Save the Railways petition had barely gained any traction with the locals. The tourists enjoyed the railways, but as my boss liked to point out, "Tourists can't vote like locals can."

I needed to either majorly increase tourism or drum up local interest in the trains, but it was easier said than done.

The locals didn't seem to care about the trains. I couldn't understand their apathy. It didn't make sense that I could possibly be the only one who cared this much about trains.

Even ignoring my somewhat unnatural obsession with them, trains meant a lot to me. They had always been a source of comfort for me.

For the year I'd lived off the island, I never stopped missing them. I shouldn't have left in the first place. Nothing good happened off the island; the worst of which was my short-lived relationship with Miles. Miles was the son of the CFO of the car company that was now invading our island, which, if it was a coincidence, was a horrible one.

I'd broken up with Miles when I came back to the island. It was my home and I couldn't stay away. He'd laughed at me when I told him I missed the more leisurely pace of the island and the comfort of the trains. He thought I was joking. He understood just about as well as he'd understood me our entire relationship—not at all.

He stopped laughing when I left him.

Now his car company was here on my island, threatening my home's way of life and the trains I loved. I was struggling to believe that was a coincidence.

I sighed and fought to push the thoughts out of my mind. They were worries for tomorrow. The work day was over, and like always, the train was here for me.

When everything else in my life felt chaotic, I loved that I could rely on the trains. They were a constant comfort, but lately they'd started providing a new kind of stress relief, too.

It was like my thoughts summoned the tunnel, my favorite part of the journey. The vibrations of the train car increased as we grew closer. Anticipation swirled through me as the vibrations steadily increased, sending a rush of heat to my core.

I loved trains in a way I knew other people would judge and look down on. It had started as a normal amount of healthy adoration, but the trains had changed things. It wasn't my fault they seemed to return my love and pay me special attention.

I shifted a little in my seat as the track continued to get bumpier, sending vibrations up through the seat and straight to my core.

I looked around my train car, making sure I was still alone, like always. Because the car at the back of the train provided a bumpier ride than most people enjoyed, no one else normally rode in it. It was part of why I loved this car.

I tried to tell myself I didn't need to do this, but it was no use. I was too worked up and could feel the train encouraging me to let go.

I slid further down in my seat before dipping my hand into the waistband of my pants, shuddering as I ran a finger over my already-damp silk panties. I moved them aside and slid a finger into my dripping pussy.

The train continued to buck on the tracks, heightening my arousal. I slowly pulled my finger out, now coated in my arousal, and moved up to my clit. Circling it the way I liked, I let out a moan. We were almost at the tunnel now, and I knew from experience it wouldn't take me long.

I quickly moved my fingers away from my clit, positioning them at my opening and paused, waiting. With my other hand, I flicked my left nipple, then my right. They were already stiff, and now they were almost painful. I pulled at one of the peaks, crying out at the sensation. Then the train was plunged into darkness, and I pushed two fingers deep inside myself.

I moaned loud enough that I had to hope they didn't hear it in the next car. The train bucked on the tracks in the tunnel, sending vibrations through the car and my seat as I finger-fucked myself, racing the train. The train was fast, but it was a long tunnel and I almost always came before the train exited the tunnel.

I rode my fingers hard, tugging at my hardened nipples one after the other, not holding back. I felt my release building and building; I was so close. I brushed my clit with my thumb, sending me tumbling over the edge of ecstasy, crying out as I rode out the waves of pleasure.

"Woooo-Wooooo" the train whistled almost as loud as my cries.

Light flooded back into the cabin as the train exited the tunnel.

I pulled my fingers out, wiping them on my soaked panties. I was going to have to change the moment I got home, as usual.

After the tunnel, the tracks evened out and the rest was a smooth ride. I preferred the bumpy ride. The island had been talking for years about fixing the rest of the track, but I hoped they never did.

Chapter Two

Gauge

This girl was going to be the death of me. She thought she was alone, and I tried not to watch her. I should be giving her privacy—I tried. Day after day I tried not to watch her, but day after day, I failed.

She was too tempting to look away from. With the way she came right on schedule every day, she was almost as reliable as a train. Some days she was quicker than others, but most of the time she came right as I burst from the tunnel.

I knew she thought she was alone, but it was hard not to feel like she was performing just for me.

Every day, the temptation to introduce myself grew stronger, but I shouldn't. Nothing about me was normal. She wouldn't want me. I told myself that every day. If I did meet her, things wouldn't go well. Despite being sure of this, I could feel my resolve weakening. I was miserable.

I wasn't being discrete about my feelings, either. Jamie had definitely noticed something was different. I wasn't sure if Rosie had yet, but since Jamie didn't keep their mouth shut, it wouldn't be long before Rosie knew.

I loved them both and knew how deeply they loved me. Neither would care that I was interested in someone else, but I didn't want them to learn I was hurting because of it. I was going to have to do a better job at hiding it.

Chapter Three

Rosie

"Don't repeat this, but I'm worried about Gauge," I told Jamie. Jamie wasn't good at keeping secrets, but they were better at reading people than I was. I also knew if I asked Gauge what was bothering him, I wouldn't get a straight answer.

"How come?" Jamie asked.

"He's been taking more shifts than usual, working too hard and hasn't been all that interested in playing around."

"I wouldn't worry about that too much. I think someone's got his engine going."

"Someone... like a passenger?" I asked.

Jamie nodded. "Seems like it. He's giving off sexually frustrated vibes, which is weird as scrapyard 'cause he's been less interested with us lately. There's gotta be someone that's caught his eye."

"You think?"

"I'd bet on it."

"Really? Maybe I should go check out the situation tomorrow."

"What are you gonna do?"

"What else? Meddle, obviously. If there is a person, I wanna see if they're receptive."

"Meaning...?"

"Have to make sure they'd fit in."

"He's going to be pissed," Jamie said, chuckling.

Chapter Four

Gauge

I had never given my passengers much thought before her, but she occupied my every waking thought. She was different; even though I knew it was a terrible idea, I wanted to meet her.

Against my better judgment, I felt hope creeping in. The pull to her was so strong I couldn't imagine it was one-sided. I wanted her. Her near daily self-pleasuring with my train was torture. I wanted to feel her coming undone around me, wanted to hear her crying out for me.

But today wouldn't be the day. I would have to catch her when I wasn't working, since it wasn't possible for me to talk to her on the job.

I was going to have to start riding the rails off shift, take Jamie or Rosie's trains, and see if she showed up. I both hoped and feared that she would. The thought that she could be riding other rails, pleasuring herself on other trains like she did on mine, drove me half crazy. She didn't know about me or how faithfully I watched her, but it still felt like something special she did only for me.

I didn't want to believe she was putting on a show for just anyone. Of course, I could ask Jamie or Rosie, but that felt like a violation of my girl's trust. It felt like this was almost a secret game between the two of us; telling the others, asking about her, felt like betraying that.

Her station was next, and when I pulled to a stop, every other thought except her left my mind.

I could feel my growing excitement, the building anticipation of getting to see *her* again. Except she wasn't the only one I recognized that boarded at her station.

There was a certain brown-haired, red-lipped, smirking seductress making her way toward my control room.

Rosie.

I couldn't believe she was here. She rarely left our apartment before noon, yet here she was, pushing her way into my control room.

Steam hissed out with my annoyance as I asked, "What are you doing here?"

"Good to see you, too. What a warm welcome. If you keep it up, I might come along more often."

"Wonderful," I deadpanned.

"You know you love me."

Of course I did. Rosie, Jamie, and I shared everything and I could say with confidence they were the only ones on the island—probably even in the world, who understood me. That didn't change how annoyed I was that she was here. I'd been trying to keep my fascination with a certain blonde passenger to myself, which wouldn't happen if Rosie rode with me.

"What are you doing here?" I asked again.

"Looking to see which passenger has your engines racing."

Tracks.

"You don't know what you're talking about, and you can't be here."

"Scrapyard. Last I checked, you could use a conductor."

I whistled out obscenities as she pulled out a conductor's hat and smoothed it down over her hair. With her red lipstick, dark eyes, and mischievous grin, she was stunning, and I was annoyed. This wasn't how this was supposed to go. Rosie wasn't supposed to get to talk to her first. *I* was the one fascinated with her. *I* was the one who wanted her.

She turned back and blew me a kiss.

One last chance.

"Come on, leave her alone. You're not jealous, are you?"

She raised an eyebrow, and I wondered if she would take the bait until she smirked and said, "So it's a woman. Wish me luck!"

Scrapyard.

I couldn't chase her down. I couldn't move. I could only watch as she made her way down the aisles and hope that Rosie would overlook my favorite passenger.

Maybe she wouldn't have the same appeal for Rosie as she did for me.

Maybe Rosie would stop before she got to my girl's car. My girl always sat in the back by herself. There was a chance Rosie wouldn't go that far. But I should've known better. When Rosie was on a mission, there was no deterring her. She was like a runaway train with no brakes.

Rosie entered the last car, and it was just her and my girl. What I wouldn't give to be in Rosie's position right now.

Rosie stopped short when she saw her and, knowing how worked up my girl got on these rides, I was curious how this was going to go.

Rosie sauntered over to her and I heard her ask, "Ticket?"

The beautiful blonde blinked, sitting up straighter, clearly confused. Understandably. For as long as she had ridden the train, no one had bothered her or asked about a ticket. She had never even seen a conductor. In fact, there wasn't usually a conductor at all.

"Chooo-choooo," I whistled a last warning to Rosie. She unsurprisingly ignored me.

My girl shrugged and riffled through her bag, found her ticket, and gave it to Rosie. Rosie held the ticket up to the light, inspecting it as though she thought it was fake.

After a few moments, Rosie smiled down at my girl, who squirmed under her attention. I was relieved when Rosie took the ticket and turned around, leaving her alone.

Chapter Five

Emma

My heart was beating out of my chest, and I had no idea why. My ticket was real, but seeing how closely the conductor had inspected it made me anxious. I felt like I'd just gotten away with something.

The conductor must have been new since the old one, whoever they were, hadn't ever made their way to the back of the train to check my ticket.

I would've been more upset about the intrusion if this conductor wasn't so pleasing to look at.

The thought would've been normal for anyone else but was odd for me. I didn't feel attraction like that, at least not for people.

It'd been longer than I could remember since anything—or anyone—besides the vibrations of the train had gotten me excited, but she was breathtaking.

With dark eyes and red lips, she exuded an energy that promised a good time if you were interested. The thought was as foreign as it was surprising, so I shook it off. It must just be that I was worked up from the train.

I was grateful she'd left me alone.

As the vibrations of the train increased, I wondered if I was being too reckless, though. No one had ever entered the car before while I'd been here, but today the conductor had. What if she came back?

What if she caught me?

The thought of her strutting back into the car and finding me writhing on my own fingers worked me up more than it should have.

Maybe she'd be horrified. Or maybe she and those delicious looking red lips would come pay me some attention.

The thought sent my fingers sliding under the waistband of my pants. I could feel the heat from my core through my panties before I pushed them aside. The thrum of the engines and the vibrations of the track ratcheted up my pleasure like they always did. It felt like the train was encouraging me, pushing me to ride it to my climax.

Nothing existed except me and the train, until I heard a clap break through my moans. My eyes shot up and found the conductor was standing a few seats away, eyes locked on me as she continued clapping.

My embarrassment rivaled my arousal as she smirked at me. I froze, wishing the train would swallow me up. I didn't want to move my fingers and risk bringing any more attention to where they were and what they were doing, even though the conductor's face left no room for doubt. She knew exactly what I was doing.

"Don't stop on my account," she mused, waving a manicured hand at me.

I didn't move, but I couldn't think of a single thing to say. There wasn't any excuse I could give for what I was doing. It barely made sense to me. There was no way I was going to be able to explain to this beautiful conductor why trains got my heart racing.

"It's not—" I started.

She waved me off, saying, "If you're going to say 'it's not what it looks like,' save it. I know what I see. But if you want a second opinion, I'm sure we could call someone else in and give you more of an audience."

"I-what?" I stuttered.

"Your choice, gorgeous. Put on a show for me, or we can get more of an audience in here."

"You can't be serious?"

She took a step forward, her eyes raking over me in a way that made me feel naked. "Want to test that theory?"

I didn't, but I wasn't sure I could do what she was asking. Sure, the vibrations from the train had me revved up and on edge, but I couldn't get myself off with an audience, could I?

"I've never done that before," I answered slowly.

"So, it's just the thrill of getting caught that does it for you?" she asked teasingly.

"The reality isn't quite like I imagined," I admitted.

"Oh?" she asked with a raised eyebrow. "And what is it you imagined?"

I blushed, thinking of my earlier fantasy, but there was no way I would be telling her about that.

She stalked forward, closing the rest of the distance between us. She stared down at me, and I shied away from meeting her eyes. She reached out, startling me as she put a finger under my chin and tilted my head up, forcing me to stare back at her.

"Let me guess... you pictured me finding you and hoped I'd help you."

"I..." I started before trailing off.

"I'll make this easy for you. Either you put on a little show for me, or we'll see what the cops think of your public display."

To my absolute embarrassment, I felt my inner walls tighten around my fingers. The threat of discovery made this even hotter.

The conductor ran a finger over my lips before saying, "Better get going if you don't want to have a lot of explaining to do at our next stop."

I knew the rails inside and out and knew the tunnel was coming up. The next stop was close after. I wasn't sure if I wanted to put on a show for her. At the very least, I wouldn't let myself acknowledge there might be some truth to me wanting to, but I knew I didn't want to have to explain myself to the cops.

The last thing I needed was for the island to hear about my unexplainable obsession with the trains. If anyone found out, it would ruin any progress I was making with the Save the Railways project. I couldn't let that happen.

Realizing I didn't quite have a choice, I slowly moved the fingers inside of me in further and then slowly back out. I tried to look away from the conductor, but her finger on my chin kept my eyes locked on hers.

"I think you need a little help if you're going to reach your destination before the train does. The train's quite fast," she said.

"Woooo-Wooooo," the train whistled loudly, seeming to agree with her.

The vibrations grew louder, almost like the train had sped up. She was right. I was running out of time.

She growled in frustration, her hand moving from beneath my chin to my throat as she pushed me back. My body hit the seat as she gave my throat a quick squeeze. I was about to protest when she pushed her knee in between my legs and ordered, "Fingers on your clit and ride my thigh like a bullet train."

I immediately moved my fingers from inside of me to my clit and ground against her thigh, letting out a moan as I rode her, her fingers still clutching my throat.

"Louder. I want the train to hear you."

"Chooo-chooo," the train whistled in agreement.

I let out another moan, louder this time.

"Faster," the conductor commanded, and I quickly complied, but it wasn't enough pressure.

I whined in frustration before answering back, "Harder."

"Glady," she replied with a wicked grin as she tightened her grip on my throat and pressed into me harder. Then we hit the tunnel, the train car went dark as I rode her hard.

My moans joined the whistles of the train. It was racing right along with me, like always. With one more hard thrust of her knee, I went barreling over the edge, crying out just as we broke through the tunnel. The fierce roar of the engine echoing my cries.

Outside the dark of the tunnel, I could see the conductor again. She grinned down at me. "I knew you had it in you. What a good girl," she purred as she pressed her thigh into my sensitive core once more, drawing another moan from my lips.

With one more quick squeeze, she moved her hand from my throat to my chin and tilted my face toward hers. Before I could move, she was there, brushing her red lips to mine in a quick, surprisingly chaste kiss.

She pulled away a moment later, saying, "Feel free to ride my rails any time." With a wink, she was gone, leaving me alone with a racing heart and wondering what the hell had just gotten into me.

Chapter Six

Gauge

After the stunt she pulled, I was dying to talk to Rosie. But like always, she knew exactly what I wanted and refused to give it to me. Instead of coming back to my control room, she ducked off at the next stop.

I was relieved to see that she at least went in a different direction from my girl. I wouldn't have been able to stop thinking about it for the rest of my shift if I knew there was a chance she was putting on a repeat performance somewhere with Rosie.

As it was, I was having a tough time concentrating on my job. I couldn't stop replaying the scene in my head for the long remaining hours of my shift. The way my girl had writhed under Rosie had my engines revved up and ready all day. It was excruciating, being so worked up and not able to do anything about it.

The fact that Rosie knew exactly what she'd done to me and exactly how I was feeling right now didn't help.

When I finally got home for the night, I whipped open the front door and was greeted with a different show. Rosie was sprawled out on the couch with Jamie's head between her thighs. She shot me a lazy grin. "About time. What took you so long?"

On another night, I might've joined in on the fun. *Tracks*, my body had been on edge all day and was begging me to, but that would be as good as letting Rosie win, and I refused.

"Get some clothes on. We need to talk."

"I can talk just fine like this," she replied, the lazy grin not leaving her face. "Unless, of course, you want to come closer and stuff my mouth full of that hard smokestack in your pants."

I felt myself getting even harder, my length jumping to attention at her address, picturing those cherry-red lips stretched wide around me. I took a half step toward her before stopping cold. She wanted to distract me, and I wasn't going to make it that easy for her.

"Maybe another time if you're good," I shot back, bending down and scooping her skirt off the ground and tossing it at her face. "Come on, Jam, take a break. I'm trying to talk to Rose."

Jamie came up for air, licking their glistening lips. "Have a good run?" they asked, their dark curly hair all mussed up from Rosie's fingers.

"Rosie didn't tell you she stopped by?"

"Is that what's got your gears grinding?" they asked turning to Rosie. "Did you leave him high and dry?"

"I didn't do anything to him," she answered, feigning innocence.

"Scrapyard."

"I didn't lay a hand on you."

"Exactly," I growled out. She laughed, pulling her skirt up tantalizingly slowly over her legs.

"Someone gonna fill me in?" Jamie asked.

I stared at Rosie, who smoothed down her skirt before returning my look and asking, "Better?"

"What the hell were you doing with her?"

"Her? Her who?" Jamie asked.

"I was curious," Rosie said with a shrug. "Don't tell me you didn't enjoy watching her squirm."

"She's not yours," I hissed out.

"Who?" Jamie asked again before quickly turning to Rosie and asking, "Wait, are we talking about Gauge's mystery passenger?"

She just grinned in answer.

"You found her?" Jamie asked. "What happened? What's she like? Tell me everything!" Jamie was bouncing with excitement; it was impossible to be mad at them when they were that freaking adorable. Even if they were clearly on Rosie's side, it wasn't their fault Rosie was so persuasive.

"I may or may not have taken her for a test ride."

Jamie laughed. "No wonder Gauge is so annoyed. Is she worth his obsession?"

"Humans don't usually do it for me. But I have to hand it to him, she was fun."

"Hope you had enough fun to last you a while, 'cause you're staying away from her now."

"Says who?"

"Me."

"And if I don't?"

"You will." I wasn't sure how I would enforce that, but Rosie and I weren't new to power struggles. I knew if I showed any sign of backing down, she'd take full advantage.

"Ughh," she groaned. "Why, though? It's not like you're having any fun with her. She doesn't even know you're there."

That wasn't fair, and she knew it. "Because I'm working!" I snapped back.

"And what's your excuse for the rest of the time?"

I didn't have one, but I couldn't admit that to Rosie. "It isn't the right time yet."

"And when will it be?" she challenged.

I paused a moment before answering decisively, "Tomorrow."

"Really?" she asked, surprised.

"What's your plan?" Jamie asked.

"I'd tell you, but I don't trust Rosie to not interfere."

It was only half true. The bigger reason I wasn't willing to tell Jamie was because I didn't actually have a plan yet.

But it was fine. Tomorrow was my day off, so I had time to come up with something.

I moved toward my bedroom, but before I could get far, Rosie asked, "Are you sure you don't want me or Jamie to help you take the edge off tonight?"

It was tempting, but I didn't want to let her win. Besides, I was pretty sure it was going to take most of the night for me to figure out a plan.

"I'm fine," I replied.

"If you're sure," Rosie taunted. "More attention for me then."

I didn't have to turn around to know she'd pulled Jamie back to her. Jamie got off on being used and was incredibly eager to please. We shared them and sometimes our own bodies with each other, but tonight I wasn't going to indulge Rosie. I wasn't in the mood.

At least that's what I told myself as I shut the door.

Unfortunately, the door wasn't thick enough to block out the whistling moans coming from the other room. I was starting to regret my decision, but I was too stubborn to let Rosie win. Instead, I continued to lie there, listening to their pleasure and thinking about my girl.

It was going to be a long night.

Chapter Seven

Emma

"How's it going out here?" I heard my boss Cassie ask.

I stifled a groan and attempted to force a smile before looking up, but I wasn't convinced I'd succeeded in more than a grimace.

It was going like shit. I'd barely slept last night; I was too busy thinking about the conductor and my little performance yesterday.

I'd woken up late and felt too nervous to take the train in case I saw her, so I'd taken a far more expensive cab here, which gave me more worries. What if someone saw me, the head of the Save the Railways project, taking a car? If anyone noticed, it might cause me trouble.

I had to get over myself. Despite what had happened yesterday with the conductor, I had to take the train home today like always. If I wanted to keep the trains running—and I desperately did—I couldn't avoid her. I would just have to face my fears of running into her.

Maybe it wouldn't be so bad, though. Maybe she wouldn't be there, or if she was, maybe she would ignore me. I just wasn't quite able to convince myself that's what I actually wanted.

Cassie cleared her throat, reminding me she'd asked a question that I hastened to answer.

"Good," I lied. "What can I do for you?"

"Stop letting your train of thought get derailed by the Railway project?"

I took a deep breath and asked, "Is that an order?"

She sighed. "No, I suppose not. You haven't been letting your other work pile up, though I have no idea how you're getting that done and being the champion of the railway at the same time."

It was easy to do both when no one wanted to hear anything about the railways. No one seemed to care. I wished I were busier. It would mean feeling like I was accomplishing more.

"I wish I had more to do," I admitted, unable to stop the defeat I was feeling from coming out. "It feels like I'm not doing enough."

Cassie lowered herself into one of the chairs facing my desk. "If the Railway project doesn't work out, it won't be because of your lack of effort. You're trying so hard."

"But it's not enough."

"If anyone can do it, it's you," she insisted, giving me a smile. "I just wish you'd turned your mind to an easier project. Defeat doesn't look good on you."

"Give it to me straight. Is it hopeless?"

"I'm not sure about hopeless. Difficult, yes, but you're good at what you do."

"You think?" I asked.

"I hired you for a reason. When you moved back to the island and came in looking for a job, I was convinced you weren't suited to the job. After all, you left. Why would someone who wanted to leave the island be good at convincing people they wanted to come visit the island? You convinced me I was wrong. You convinced me that, because you tried to leave and *had* to come back, you were the perfect person to convince others about the draw the island has and to get tourists lining up to come."

I smiled a little at her words.

"And you were right. Our numbers are up from this time last year."

"Not by much," I argued.

"But enough to show you're making a difference, and there's so many people commenting about coming later in the year. Don't forget, most of the island's hotels are completely booked for the fall festival and the Halloween festival that didn't even exist before you."

I shrugged, fighting back the blush I felt coming on. "It was nothing; just doing my job."

"Exactly. So, like I said, if anyone can stand up to big car-ma, it's you."

I chuckled at that. It was a dumb play on words, comparing the car industry with the pharmaceutical industry in their relentless drive for profit over community.

It was nice to know Cassie was in my corner, even if I didn't think she understood why the trains were so important to me. I barely understood myself, but Cassie's playful, teasing support warmed my heart.

"Big car-ma will get their karma," I joked.

She grinned. "There she is. Confidence suits you, and you'll need it for where I'm sending you."

"Where's that?"

"It's not the where, but the who. I arranged a meeting for you with one of the higher ups at big car-ma."

"Why?" I asked quickly.

"Because the Railway project is important to you. I figured maybe you can try to find out what they want. See if compromise is possible."

I thanked her as much as I was able to, but I had a bad feeling about this. I doubted the meeting would be with Miles's father himself, but I knew the type very well and doubted they'd be receptive to the plight of the trains.

I couldn't help feeling panicked, like I was caught on a runaway train.

Chapter Eight

Gauge

So much for my plans. I'd been riding Jamie's train all day hoping to see her, but she hadn't been there this morning. A ridiculous part of me wondered if she didn't use the rails this morning because she knew it wasn't going to be me driving her. But of course, that was crazy.

Still, she wasn't there, despite *always* being here. Maybe Rosie spooked her. That was the more likely reason, even I wanted it to be about me.

I would give it another few stops and then I'd give up for the day. Go home and forget about my foolish plan... at least until my next day off.

I knew I couldn't ignore the pull I felt to her forever, especially now that Rosie had touched her. It shouldn't been have Rosie—it should have been me. Maybe it could be if I talked to her. If I didn't try, I knew I'd regret it.

Her afternoon station was next. I knew it wasn't time for her to be coming back yet, but I was feeling a bit stalker-ish waiting for her. If she wasn't there now, I'd call it a day and go home.

. From the sighs of their engine and huffs of their whistles, I knew Jamie was judging and mocking me. I couldn't really blame them. I didn't get like this over anyone. I didn't pine, and contrary to what I knew they were thinking; I didn't mope. They were right, though—I was being ridiculous. If she wasn't here, I was going to go home.

I left the control room, moving through the cars toward the back of the train. I knew if she was going to board the train, that's where she would go.

The train was much busier than mine had been. If she was about to board, she wasn't going to enjoy not being alone. I picked a seat, making sure there were open seats all around me, and waited.

When the doors opened, to my shocked delight, she was there.

I could barely hold back my excitement as she looked around the car, trying to decide where to sit. There were a few other people in the car. While it wasn't crowded, it wasn't deserted like her usual car on my train. She wouldn't be able to lose herself to the rhythm of the rails like she normally did. From the slight frown on her face, she had to be thinking the same, although she seemed more distracted than usual. I felt a slight smile on my face when she noticed me.

She wouldn't recognize me, of course, having never actually seen me off the clock, but her eyes stopped on mine just the same.

I widened my smile a bit, delighted when a tentative one crossed her face.

It seemed like she crossed the cabin without consciously meaning to, since she blinked in surprise once she was standing in front of me.

She brushed a stray hair from her face before nodding to the seat next to me. "Anyone sitting there?"

I grinned wider at her and answered, "No, it's all yours."

Once she sat beside me, I held out my hand. "I'm Gauge."

"Emma," she said, shaking my hand with a slight smile. After a moment, she asked, "Weird question, but I'm headed to an important meeting and kind of freaking out about it. Can I practice my pitch on you?"

My lips curved up in amusement. She was always alone on my train, so I'd never heard her speak this many words. I don't know what I expected, but this fast-talking bundle of energy was a surprise.

"Sure. Happy to do anything I can do to help a gorgeous woman."

Emma blushed a little before rushing to continue. "Thank you. So, I'm meeting with someone high up at the new car company on the island about their motorway initiative. I don't know who I'm meeting with, but it hardly matters—I know the type and I know it's going to be hard. I can't let this go, though. The trains are the backbone of the island. Without the trains, the island isn't home."

I straightened up a little at that, preening under the compliment. "The trains are special here."

Her blush deepened as she quickly nodded. "They are. Which is why I have to swallow my pride and meet with Big Car-ma. I've got to see if there's anything I can do to get them to change their minds. The trains are too important."

"The trains make the island special," I agreed.

Emma grinned, turning and surprising me by squeezing my arm. "I'm so glad someone else agrees with me! It's why this meeting is so important. The car company wants to do away with the trains."

I froze; sure I didn't hear her right. Or if I did, perhaps I was misunderstanding. "What do you mean, do away with the trains?"

"It's terrible!" she rushed on. "They want to sweep in with their motorways and their cars and make the trains obsolete. It won't happen quickly, of course. But eventually, if we let them get a stronger foothold on the island, the cars will make trains a thing of the past. They'll shut down the tracks and send these beautiful machines to the scrapyard."

The scrapyard. My engine stopped, oil running cold at the thought. It wasn't possible for the tracks to be shut down, was it?

The thought of Jamie, Rosie and I rusting in a scrapyard was enough to drive the thoughts of seducing the woman before me from my mind.

Of course, I was being dramatic. That would never happen to us. We'd leave before we let ourselves go to rust in a scrapyard, but it was an unsettling thought. I loved the island. It felt like home and I didn't want to leave.

Emma must have noticed a change on my face. Squeezing my hand, she quickly reassured me, "Don't worry. I won't let them take away my home like that."

There was something about the way she said it, despite how worried she'd seemed just a moment ago, which made me believe her. There was a determination in her eyes that made me believe the world would bow at her feet if she asked it to.

"You know something?" I asked. She tilted her head in question, so I continued. "There's something about you that makes me believe you could do anything you set your mind to. I'm just glad, for the island's sake, that you find the trains a worthy cause."

The red of her flushed cheeks was quickly becoming my new favorite color. "I'm glad someone else cares. It's been really hard to find people who care enough to pledge to help."

Even if I hadn't cared about the trains, which of course I did, I knew this was the opportunity I'd been looking for. Helping her—and myself, Jamie, and Rosie in the process—would give me a reason to have to spend more time with her.

Even if I hadn't been personally invested in Emma's goals, this would've been perfect. As it was, though, she had lucked into meeting perhaps the one person—besides Jamie and Rosie, of course—who was as invested as she was in making sure nothing changed with the trains.

"I'll help however I can," I said quickly. "Why don't you take my number? You can let me know how the meeting goes and how I can help."

"That would be great. I would ask if you're sure, but I'm desperate enough for help that I won't give you a chance to change your mind," Emma replied, laughing as she pulled out her phone and handed it to me.

Jamie had insisted we learn to use the human technology, and I'd never been more grateful than in this moment. When Jamie had insisted on phones, I'd scoffed, thinking there was no chance in hell I'd ever need to know how to use one. After all, I lived with Rosie and Jamie, and couldn't care less about communicating with humans.

As I typed in my number and shot myself a quick text so I'd have hers, I hoped Jamie wasn't listening. If they knew how right they were, I would never hear the end of it.

Chapter Nine

Gauge

I should have gotten off at the next stop instead of listening to Jamie's whistles and heading to the control room.

They still would've given me a hard time at home, but at least I would've had a breather before they tried to squeeze more information out of me.

"Come on, dude, you have to give me more than that," Jamie whined.

"You probably heard everything. There's nothing else to tell."

"I barely heard anything. Come on, tell me about her. She doesn't usually ride my rails."

I felt a little smug about that. Apparently, I wasn't the only one who noticed Emma usually just rode mine. Even though it probably had more to do with convenience and her schedule than anything, it made me feel special.

"Not my fault she has good taste."

"Can't fault her. You do taste good."

I laughed. "You would know."

"You think she'd drive you crazy like I do?"

I paused, not sure what to say or whether to admit to the fantasies and dreams I'd been having about her.

"I'm not jealous, if that's what you're worried about," they said with a whistling laugh.

They were right. I was being ridiculous, and they sounded sincere in their curiosity.

"With all the times she's gotten herself off on my seats, I can't stop thinking about her."

Jamie laughed again. "You think she knows you're watching her?"

"Of course not," I answered quickly, even if I wished she did. "She's driving me crazy, though."

"You think she'd ride you like she does your seats?"

Rails, I hoped so. "We'll see now, won't we?"

"You think Rosie'll be jealous?"

Screw Rosie and her jealousy. Even if she was, she had no right to screw my girl on my train. Emma didn't know what she was doing to drive me mad, but Rosie did and had loved every second of it.

"I hope she is. Scrapyard, I'd fuck her in front of Rosie if she let me."

"Seems like she might be into that," Jamie commented.

Well, my dreams were going to be even more tortuous now with that image in my head.

Chapter Ten

Emma

Gauge had been a welcome distraction, but I couldn't let myself stay that way. It was a nice reminder, though, that I wasn't the only one who cared. There were probably more people on the island just like him who cared about the trains, too. Well, not *just* like him; I amended the thought after remembering how handsome he was.

It was shaping up to be a weird week for me since he was the second person to catch my attention. He was striking, though.

With his perfectly tousled black hair, dark eyes, and tall lean body, I had a hard time thinking there was anyone out there just like him. But I was sure there were less beautiful people out there who cared, too, and that was enough for me to stroll into the meeting at the town hall with a bounce to my step and a confidence I'd been missing when I left the office. Unfortunately, my confidence quickly dissolved when I saw who was waiting for me in the conference room.

This had to be a cruel joke.

Maybe I'd fallen onto the track and been sliced clean in half before I'd even boarded the train. That would make more sense than this hell being reality, because sitting across from me with a smug look on his arrogant face was my ex-boyfriend, Miles.

The last time I'd seen him, I'd informed him that he would never matter to me like the trains and my island did. He'd sworn I'd regret leaving him. I hadn't believed him for a second, but now that he was here, I began to wonder if he'd been threatening me.

"Miles? What are you doing here?"

"Nice to see you again too, Emmy," he replied, looking smug while using the nickname he knew I hated.

"Yeah um—nice," I faltered. Not exactly the word I would have picked. "But what are you doing here?"

"Well, you know who my family is."

I knew his dad was a CFO of the company, but I didn't know Miles was so involved with the motorway initiative on the island. "I know your dad is a CFO—"

"Actually, he's the CEO now," he interrupted before I could continue, "making me his CFO. Isn't that great?"

I wasn't sure what to say. Things hadn't ended well. On top of how bad the breakup was, he never liked the island. It was something I thought I could move past, but I was wrong. The island was a part of me; when I felt it calling me back, I didn't think twice about leaving him.

"Funny, isn't it? How you left me for this backwards island and now I'm here to help bring it into the future?"

Again, funny isn't the word I would use. Miles couldn't be serious. If he knew anything about me, it was how much this island meant to me.

"I'm not sure what to say."

"I've never heard you at a loss for words before. You must be just so happy to see me here. After all, you dumped me since I wouldn't agree to come back to your backwards, ridiculous, little island, and now here I am. You must be overjoyed."

"I'm confused." I paused for a second, letting my brain catch up to what he wasn't saying. He was pushing me to see if I would play along. He expected me to agree. It was how our relationship had played out, so it made sense, and since I was here to schmooze whoever was in charge, it couldn't hurt.

"Of course I'm happy you're here," I continued. "I'm just confused. What are you doing here?"

"Well, when you left me for the island, it made me think it must be a special place. If it was special enough for you to dump me, maybe it was somewhere I wanted to pay attention to." He looked like he was being sincere, but I knew what he was really driving at. The motorway initiative was my fault. He was bringing his car company to my island to hurt me. He knew how much I loved the nostalgic atmosphere and relaxed pace of life on the island, and most importantly, the reliance on trains. The reliability of the trains, and by extension the reliability of the island, could be counted on by everyone.

Now Miles was trying to pull the rug out from under me with this motorway initiative. There was no other way to look at it. I wasn't naïve enough to believe the financial gain on the island was enough for his company to be here. This was personal. He was lashing out at me for how I had surprised him by ending our relationship. My heart sank at the realization that this was going to be so much more difficult than I'd thought, and I already believed it was going to be near impossible.

Regardless of what he was saying, Miles was here to make me miserable, and it was working. He wasn't the cold-hearted executive who would only listen to cold hard facts and money like I had anticipated. He was worse. He had revenge on his mind and wasn't going to listen to reason, no matter how legitimate it was.

"It's a special place to me."

"And you're a special girl to me," he tutted, looking so smug I wanted to smack him.

"I can't believe you did all this for me."

The sparkle in his eye had anger and worry warring in my gut. I had to give my original strategy a shot, though. "Are you running the project?" I asked.

He nodded. "When I told my father about you and the island, he agreed it would be good experience for me."

"I can't believe it," I mused, hoping he wouldn't see through my tone. "No one's ever taken a financial loss for me before." The amusement fell from his face, and I didn't need to fake my smile as I continued, "It's so romantic!"

Miles recovered a bit of his earlier arrogance and argued, "I've always been a romantic, but it won't be a loss. It's a win-win; I'm here for you and it'll benefit the company. There's plenty of potential for expansion once we dig up the railways and build more motorways. People will be lining up to get cars—trains are the transportation of the past. I know you like how simple they are, but you don't have to worry. I'll make sure you never have to bother to learn to drive yourself."

I held tight to the binder I had brought, squeezing it hard. I couldn't believe him. The utter arrogance of this man. I couldn't believe I'd ever been with him.

"Why can't the cars and trains coexist?" I asked through gritted teeth and a forced smile.

"The trains take up way too much room. The tracks are all over the island. People are living in the past; cars are so much more convenient. At least they will be, once we get the trains out of the way."

"If you do that, you'll take away everything special about this island."

Miles rolled his eyes before giving me a condescending smile. "You and those trains. It's almost as if you like them more than people."

I swallowed, hoping he didn't know how close he'd actually come to the truth. Besides Gauge and the conductor, who were weird outliers, trains were the thing that got my heart racing. I didn't understand it and didn't have the time or money for enough therapy to unpack it, but that didn't make it untrue.

Sure, there might be something wrong with me. But with my ex-boyfriend staring down at me condescendingly, judging me for not wanting to introduce more chaotic transportation and pollution to the island, maybe it made sense I was choosing the trains over this conceited car salesman.

"More than some people," I agreed.

"Well, better get your goodbyes in quick since we're green lighting the project in two weeks."

"Two weeks?!" I exclaimed.

"It was the fastest we could get the necessary permits."

I couldn't believe he'd gotten them so quickly. I had no idea how I was possibly going to raise the local support needed to save the trains in that short a time, especially when it sounds like he'd already called his daddy to grease the right palms.

But I wasn't giving up without a fight.

I turned on my heel and grabbed the door handle. Before I could leave, he added, "Don't worry, Emmy. When the trains leave you, I'll still be here to comfort you."

"I would rather get run over by one of your stupid cars," I hissed under my breath. It was stupid, reckless, and unfortunately not quiet enough that he didn't hear.

"Don't bother with the dramatics. It won't change anything. The trains are going to get torn apart either way, but if you keep up this ice princess act, I might not be waiting when you try to come crawling back."

I stormed out, seething too much to respond.

Chapter Eleven

Emma

I had been planning to go back to work, but I couldn't bear the thought of telling Cassie all about what happened, so instead I took the first train home.

It wasn't my usual train, but the ride was uneventful, anyway. I was too deep in my own head to lose myself to the pleasure of the rails like I usually did. Every bump and jolt of the track felt like an accusation, like a jab at me and my failures. If the trains were destroyed, I would be the reason. Me and my terrible taste in men were going to destroy the island I loved.

I had to do something about it, but I had no idea what.

My usual wine, ice cream and reality show binging weren't doing the trick to lift my spirits. I was too upset and worked up worrying about the trains.

It felt like the world was ending, or at least, that it would on the island without the trains. Wouldn't the island be devastated to lose the trains? Or was Miles right, and I was the only one who cared about them? Would everyone be fine with having to switch to cars even if they were a more expensive, less reliable means of transportation?

I almost called Cassie for advice when I spotted Gauge's name in my phone. He cared about the trains, too. I wasn't alone.

I clearly was insane, though, since I hit the call button before I could think better of it. I hung up almost immediately, but not quickly enough. since he called right back. I stared in horror as my phone began to ring with his immediate call back.

I couldn't answer. I hardly knew him, but not answering after I'd called him first was also really rude.

I settled on a cop-out, hitting reject and texting him instead.

> I'm so sorry, didn't mean to call!

The response came almost instantaneously.

Gauge

> Don't worry about it! But now that we're talking, how'd your meeting go?

I wasn't sure what to tell him. I barely knew him, but it was nice knowing someone else cared about me. No, about *the trains*, I corrected myself. He cares about the trains, not me. It was nice to not be alone in that. Even Cassie, whose texts I hadn't been able to force myself to return after the meeting, only really cared about the trains because she cared about me. Gauge, though, actually cared about the machines themselves.

Honestly?

Gauge

I'll take whatever I can get

The joke made me actually laugh out loud. Maybe it wasn't that stupid of me to have texted him after all.

Truthfully, it didn't go great

Gauge

I doubt that's true

I sighed, unsure how to explain that my ex was spearheading the project. I wasn't even sure I wanted to. I ended up settling for a simpler version of the truth.

The guy running the project has it out for me

Gauge

What's his problem?

He hates trains

And fun

And me

More me than anything

We dated for a while

Gauge

…You dated someone who hates trains?

I laughed loudly at that before quickly replying.

I know, I know, horrible taste

Gauge

Have things changed?

Now that I know he hates trains? Of course, I can't stand him

Gauge

Because of the trains?

I was smiling at my phone now. Gauge had a great sense of humor.

It's not alllll about the trains

Gauge

But it's sort of about the trains

Yeahhhh - it's sort of about the trains

Gauge

Bit of a rail rider?

I blushed at his words, wondering if he had some way of knowing how accurate that was.

Something like that

Gauge

Good to know

Gauge

But that's actually not what I meant

Huh?

Gauge

I meant, do you have better taste now?

I was so glad he couldn't see how red my face was. Of course he wasn't talking about the trains. *Did* I have better taste now? I hadn't been with anyone since Miles. No one had really interested me. Although, Miles hadn't either, but that hadn't stopped me.

Couldn't say, haven't been with anyone since

I wasn't sure why I was being so honest with Gauge. He was nice, and distractingly handsome, but he was a stranger. Maybe that's why it was so easy to talk to him.

Gauge

What do you say we go grab a drink? Take your mind off things?

I considered it, but the wine I'd already consumed hadn't helped and I didn't really want to leave my house. He was right, though. I needed a way to work out my frustration. I needed to do something to get Miles and his crusade against the trains off my mind.

> ...Or you could come over?

I couldn't believe I'd sent the message, but when his reply came through...

Gauge

> Give me a time and place

I couldn't bring myself to regret it.

What I *did* regret was only giving myself thirty minutes to make me and my apartment look guest ready.

After five minutes, I abandoned the pretense of cleaning and put on a new pink lingerie set and a little bit of makeup. There wasn't time for much else since he'd be there before I knew it. I was shocked to find that I was excited, not anxious. Before my encounter with the conductor, I hadn't been worked up by anything besides riding the rails in longer than I could remember.

Maybe Gauge would be good for me, and if not, I could always work out my frustrations riding my favorite train tomorrow.

Chapter Twelve

Gauge

There was a small chance I was misinterpreting her message, but I doubted I was the only one that felt the chemistry between us.

Emma had no idea how long I'd been watching her and how often I'd seen her face twisted in ecstasy, but she'd invited me over at ten at night to her house. There weren't many other ways to interpret that.

I'd basically ran out the door when she told me, but I wasn't quick enough to escape either Rosie or Jamie's notice. I saw them exchange a knowing look before I closed the door in their faces. I didn't want to hear what they had to say right now. I was too excited.

I'd been pacing around Emma's neighborhood for the last ten minutes. I thought it would take me longer to get from our warehouse apartment in the train yard to her apartment downtown, but I'd practically sprinted the whole way and didn't want to make her anxious by showing up early.

The moment my phone chimed ten, I pulled open the door, made my way up two flights of stairs to her landing, and knocked on her door.

Before I even pulled my hand away, the door opened. The lighting was low in her apartment, but it looked neat and cozy. It was the opposite of our warehouse apartment, which was always loud and chaotic.

Emma held the door open from behind, so it wasn't until I stepped in and she closed the door that I saw what she was wearing. Actually, how *little* she was wearing.

She was wearing a tiny, pink, strappy bra with an even smaller thong.

If I wasn't sure about why she had invited me over, her outfit was a sign that I couldn't misread. It became especially apparent when she slipped her hands down her body to the strings of her thong on her hips. My greedy eyes followed her, unwilling to take more than she was offering. She caressed the strings as she asked, "What do you say? I could use a distraction. Wanna take me for a ride?"

I closed the distance in less than a heartbeat, pressing her against the door. As my lips crashed onto hers, I reached behind her to undo her bra when I felt her hands on the hem of my shirt.

Tracks, I couldn't let her see that much of me. Humans tended to be weird about our markings—at least, that's what Rosie had told me. I pulled away from Emma, far enough to give her a cocky grin, and murmured, "I didn't say you could touch."

I spun her around, pressing her face against the door. I grabbed her hands and held them in mine, using my other hand to unbuckle my belt.

She jumped at the snap of my belt as I pulled it through the loops of my jeans. "What are you doing?"

I paused and answered her question with one of my own. "Do you trust your conductor?"

I was prepared to wait for her to consider it, but Emma's answer came quickly, instinctually. "Yes."

"Well then, let's get you buckled up 'cause it's going to be a hell of a ride," I said as I sank to my knees behind her, putting me at eye level with her bra clasp. Ignoring that for now, I wrapped my belt around her wrists, yanking it tight.

"Oof."

"Too tight?"

"I've felt worse."

I chuckled, thinking how much Rosie and Jamie would get a kick out of the apparently bratty Emma. Just for that, I yanked it tighter before buckling the makeshift restraint in place, binding her wrists together.

I felt her testing them and was proud, but not surprised, when her wrists weren't able to separate. Rosie and I liked our restraints.

"You can squirm all you like," I taunted as I ran one of my hands up the inside of her leg.

I laughed when she instantly parted for me. I brushed a knuckle over the tiny fabric she called underwear and grinned at how soaked they were. I'd barely even touched her, but she was damn near aching and ready for me.

I moved my hand back down to the inside of her thigh, causing her to whimper.

"Patience," I teased. "We have a few more stops before your destination." I leaned forward, taking her bra clasp in my mouth and after a few moments, I felt it give under my teeth and pulled back. I slowly rose, licking and kissing my way up her back and neck to her ear. I grazed it with my teeth as my hand pulled one of her straps down and then the other.

I moved my hands to her front and pulled her bra down to her stomach, freeing her breasts. It wouldn't go further with her hands bound, but that was as far as I needed it to go.

I was tempted to spin her back around so I could have a better look at her, but I didn't want to risk her seeing more of me. Instead, I pressed myself into her ass as I moved my hands up to explore her chest. I ground into her as I flicked one of her nipples and was rewarded with a moan. I earned more by kissing and licking my way up her neck.

I was tempted to mark her like Rosie sometimes did to Jamie, but I didn't know if she'd like it, so I held myself back.

I felt, and knew she could too, that the smokestack in my pants was harder than coal. From the way she was grinding back against me, she was as impatient as I was.

"I'd say it's almost time for your train to arrive, don't you?"

Emma whined, making me laugh.

She was squirming against me, but what little there was of her panties were still in my way. I sunk to my knees again and ran my fingers over the fabric on her hips. "Let's finish getting you ready."

"I've been ready," she whined breathlessly.

I grabbed the straps and yanked her thong down her legs. Rising to my feet, I pressed my thigh between her legs, forcing them apart. I ground into her core as I pushed my jeans down, freeing the hard pipe in my pants.

I stroked the length a few times and felt it swell even more. Knowing she was as ready for me as she was going to get, I turned slightly, moving my thigh and positioning my length between her legs.

"I'm going to bury my train so far in your tunnel," I growled.

"All aboard," she answered around a moan. *Engines*, my girl was perfect.

I pushed my length inside of her, slowly at first, not sure if she would be able to take all of me. But when she whined out, "Fuck my tunnel hard," I lost control. I rammed the rest of my length into her, feeling her inner walls tighten around me as I moved in and out of her.

Her moans ramped up, and I was fighting hard to hold back the whistling noises threatening to come out of me. I groaned, feeling steam start to come out of my ears, and knew I was close.

"Last stop's coming up," I told her.

"I'm almost there," Emma whined. Of course she was. My girl was right on schedule, like always.

With a few more thrusts, I couldn't hold back anymore and let out a loud "Wooo-Wooo," filling up her tunnel with my steam. From how loudly she cried out, she arrived at the same time.

After a few moments of hard breathing, I slowly pulled out of her and tucked my pipe back in my pants, then got to work freeing her hands from my belt.

After releasing her, Emma turned around, moving past me toward her couch. She grabbed a robe and draped it over herself before turning back around. "That was..." She paused, rubbing her wrists.

I quickly took her wrists in my hands. "Did I hurt you?" I asked gently rubbing them.

"No, no, I'm fine," she said quickly. "That was just...wow."

"You were pretty 'wow' yourself," I replied with a smirk that turned into a grin when she laughed.

"I'm so glad you came."

"Glad I could get you there, too."

She laughed again, and it sounded like music. "That wasn't what I meant, but that works, too. Do you have to get going?" she asked.

"Do you want me to leave?"

Emma reddened. "Huh? No, sorry, I just meant 'cause your phone went off."

I raised an eyebrow in confusion. "It did?"

"The train noises we heard a few minutes ago. I figured someone was calling you."

That would take a lot less explaining, so I fished my phone out of my pocket. Pretending to check it, I replied, "Yeah, it's one of my roommates wondering when I'll be back."

"Oh geez, sorry. This was crazy. I should let you go home. I have work pretty early in the morning, anyway."

I was surprised at the quick dismissal. It must've shown on my face because she quickly added, "Tomorrow's Friday, though, so I'll be off work for the weekend. We could go on a real date... if you want to."

"You read my mind," I said quickly. "I'd love to spend more time with you."

I wanted to get to know Emma inside and out. I was determined to make her fall for me as hard as I'd already fallen for her.

"Maybe at your place this time?" she asked.

"Don't want me back at your place?" I chuckled.

"No, no, it's not that!" she quickly protested. "It's just that we were probably a bit loud. Maybe your place would be better? If your roommates aren't around?"

"I'll make sure they're not a problem," I told her, though I wasn't positive I could deliver on that. Rosie and Jamie would be near impossible to force out of the house if they knew I was having Emma over.

Maybe I could just get them to agree to stay quiet. Rosie had to see that if we wanted to share Emma eventually, which I'd be willing to do if she was into it, we didn't want to scare her off.

We had to take it slow; all three of us spending time with her at the apartment would be the opposite of easing her into things.

"See you tomorrow," Emma said with an adorably shy smile as she shut the door behind me.

The only way I was able to force myself to go back home was because I knew I'd get to see her again tomorrow.

As I walked home, I floated idea after idea in my mind about how to convince Rosie and Jamie to either be cool or make themselves scarce. I started to worry there wouldn't be enough time to convince them. I wasn't even sure it was possible, since Rosie and Jamie seemed just as intrigued by her as I was, but I would try.

Chapter Thirteen

Emma

"Soooo..." Cassie said as she came over to my desk. "I'm guessing based on the lack of updates that things didn't go so well yesterday?"

"Take whatever your worst possible scenario was and double it."

"Oh, honey, what happened?"

"The executive I was meeting with? He turned out to be my ex-boyfriend," I groaned.

Her eyes widened. "No!!"

"Yes!! It was horrible!"

"What's he doing here?" Cassie asked skeptically.

"Making me miserable."

She scoffed. "Besides that. I'm sure there's another reason he's here."

"No, seriously. He said he picked the island to make me miserable."

"Did he really?"

I paused before clarifying, "Well, not in those words. But it was clear that was what he meant. He said he picked the island because of me, and because it was so special to me that it must be a special place."

"That sounds...nice?" she asked, clearly confused.

"Trust me, it's not," I argued. "He's pissed I left him to come home and wants to get back at me."

"So, he's basing his business decisions and financial future around getting revenge against you?"

"It's crazy! How can I possibly reason with crazy?"

"Doesn't sound like you can."

"Exactly!" I huffed. "But if I don't, by the time he realizes I was right and he's wasting time and money on the island, it'll already be too late for the trains."

"I didn't take you for a quitter," Cassie challenged.

My heart leapt into my throat at that as I forced out a reply. "What? I'm not, but what else can I do? I don't have his money or influence."

"But he doesn't have your drive and determination, or your passion for this island and the trains," Cassie insisted.

I fought to keep my face neutral at the "passion for the trains" comment, but she wasn't wrong about that, or any of the other things she'd said.

Maybe there was something to do. I gathered up my binder with my flyers and petition in it and said, "You're right. I needed that, thank you."

"You've got this!" she encouraged me as I headed out the door. "And don't worry! If today doesn't work, you'll have the whole weekend to brainstorm."

I laughed at that, replying, "So glad you believe in me," as I exited.

Chapter Fourteen

Gauge

Are you around?

My phone was plugged into the train console, so Emma's message flashed across the screen, making sure I didn't miss it. Unfortunately, I had to disappoint her. I had a few more hours of work before I could go home.

I'm stuck at work. Sorry, what's going on?

Her response wasn't immediate. In fact, it took long enough that I started to wonder if I should be worried.

I'm fine, just a weird situation with an ex - was hoping for a rescue

I responded almost as quickly as I thought it.

> Are you safe??

Emma

> Yes!

Emma

> I'm fine, don't worry

Emma

> Just could use an excuse to get out of here -
> he knows where I live so I don't really want
> to go home

An idea struck, but I wasn't sure if it was a crazy one. I paused a moment before deciding it probably couldn't hurt.

> I'm not around yet, but my roommate is.
> They could come get you and you could
> hang out with them until I'm off?

Emma

> You don't have to do that, I'm really okay.
> I'm sorry for bugging you

> It's no problem really, I'm sure they'd be
> happy to

A little too happy, unfortunately, but I wasn't sure what else to do. She probably would've met Jamie tonight, anyway. This was just speeding up the process.

Besides, me and Rosie had both already met and bonded with her—if you counted Rosie fucking her on my train as bonding. It was probably only fair to give Jamie a chance to get to know her.

I shot them a quick text, explaining the situation. As I expected, they were too eager to oblige, but the relief I could sense on my girl even through her texts made me sure it was the right decision.

Chapter Fifteen

Emma

I checked my phone again for what had to be at least the tenth time in the last few minutes.

This wasn't how today was supposed to go. I was supposed to be brave and determined. Instead, I'd gotten to the town center, prepared to canvass the streets for signatures on my Save the Railways project, and saw Miles was out there doing the same thing. Except where people mostly ignored me, it seemed like they were interested in what he had to say.

He winked and waved at me from where he was holding court, surrounded by people, and I couldn't do it anymore.

I wanted to go home, but he knew where I lived. I didn't know what else to do, so I'd texted Gauge.

It was a little pathetic of me, but now I was waiting for his roommate to come rescue me like a damsel in distress. So much for me being driven and determined.

"Emma?"

I looked up and was surprised to see an adorably dorky-looking person with dark curly hair falling in their eyes. They pushed it off their face with a lopsided grin that I feel a little in love with on the spot.

"You're Emma, right?" they asked again, and I quickly nodded.

"Yeah, sorry, are you Gauge's roommate?"

"Yeah, I'm Jamie. Good to meet you."

"You too. How'd you know it was me?"

"Easy! Gauge told me to look for the most beautiful woman in the square, and..." They made a show of looking around and I followed their eyes, taking in the rest of the square. Besides my ex and the group of people he was talking to, there were a few businessmen walking through the area, some parents with their kids, and a few elderly women.

They raised their eyebrows at me, not bothering to finish the sentence, and I laughed.

"Fair enough. Probably wasn't too hard to find."

"He wasn't wrong about you, though. Even if the square were full, you would've stood out."

I had no idea what to say to that, so instead, I shifted the topic. "Thank you for coming to get me. I felt ridiculous, but I didn't want to go home."

"Is he dangerous?" they asked, a calculating look on their face.

"No, no, nothing like that. Just a jerk that I don't have the time or energy to deal with."

"Preach. Let's get you out of here then. Our place is at the train yard, but we don't have to head straight there if you have anything else you need or want to do."

"Like what?"

"We could grab some apps and a drink if you want? Sounds like today was rough. You can dish all about this messy breakup of yours, or if you'd prefer a distraction, I've been told I'm obnoxiously talkative."

I laughed at that, asking, "Who told you that?"

"Our other roommate, Rosie. She's scary beautiful, drop-dead gorgeous in a 'make your heart stop' sort of way, and domineering—but she's not wrong."

"So, you are two...?" I trailed off, not knowing what label to use.

"Fucking? Every chance I get."

I burst out laughing at that. "Wasn't quite what I was going to ask."

"But was definitely what you were wondering."

I could feel my cheeks flush. "I have a feeling if we keep talking, I'm gonna need that drink."

They laughed at that, looping their arm through mine and directing me away from my ex and the square. "Now you're talking. Gauge will love that we're bonding." Their face had a dazzlingly impish grin which implied they were trouble. Another person would've probably declined their invitation, but I was me, and I didn't shy away from a little trouble.

Chapter Sixteen

Gauge

The rest of my shift was spent almost exclusively worrying about how things were going with Emma and Jamie. I hoped they were having a good time, but I kept wondering how much Jamie was telling her.

I was grateful when Rosie finally showed up to relieve me.

Instead of actually talking, I just nodded to her and raced home.

When I got there and opened the door, Jamie and Emma were cuddled up on our couch. Jamie was sprawled out, with their head resting in Emma's lap as she stroked Jamie's hair. Emma must've been telling them something funny since Jamie burst into laughter which cut off too abruptly when I cleared my throat and they saw me.

Jamie shot me a sly grin that was as cute as it was concerning, but my girl took my attention away.

"Gauge!" she cried.

I had to laugh when she gently pushed Jamie's head off her lap so she could hop up from the couch. Then she bounded over to me and hugged me.

Her energy made it clear she'd probably had a drink or two, but I was glad she was happy and comfortable with me and Jamie.

I wrapped my arms around her and quietly asked, "Good day?"

"Much better. Thank you so much!" She pulled away, smiling at me. "I didn't mean to trouble either of you."

"No trouble at all," Jamie assured her before I could.

"I did want to talk to you, though," she said with some hesitation.

"My fault, actually," Jamie interrupted. "I kissed her and made things weird."

Emma immediately tensed. I turned to glare at Jamie, asking, "Consensually?"

"Of course!" they exclaimed. "You know me better than that."

I did. They were damn good at doing what they were told, and they were a massive flirt, but they didn't usually do anything without being directed. They were very good at taking direction, though, and at taking a good fucking.

"I'm sorry," Emma said to me. "I drank a bit more than I normally do. It was a really rough day, and I wasn't thinking."

I was struggling to decide if she felt weird about it because she thought I would be upset or because she felt weird about it happening. "Did you like it?" I asked.

"What?" Emma stuttered. "Um—I—"

"Come on, G," Jamie said, "you're stressing her out for no reason."

"What?"

Jamie rolled their eyes and turned to Emma. "Gauge is poly, and sometimes not the best at remembering that monogamy exists and that he should tell people he's poly from the start."

That was an understatement. I didn't remember to tell people because I didn't ever do this with humans. But Jamie was apparently right, since the tension in Emma's face morphed from stress into interest.

"So... wait. You two," she said, pointing between me and Jamie, "are...?"

Jamie laughed. "Yeah, us and our third roommate, the scary hot one I was telling you about, are partners."

"Really?" she asked, turning back to me.

"Yes, I'm sorry. Jamie's right, I'm somewhat new to this. I didn't think to tell you. I hope it's okay," I offered.

"Okay?" she asked in disbelief. I panicked for a moment before she continued, "Oh thank god."

"So, is it okay?" I asked.

"Does that mean you'd be okay with me kissing Jamie again?"

"I'd be okay with you fucking Jamie if you wanted, as long as I got to be involved sometimes," I answered honestly.

My mind started to run away with the possibilities, which Emma interrupted by kissing me.

I yanked her toward me, deepening the kiss for a moment before remembering we were having an important conversation and pulling away.

"So, we're okay?" I asked.

"More than okay. You're perfect," she answered, grinning.

"What about me?" Jamie asked.

"You're pretty alright," she shot back, making me chuckle.

"Ouch!" Jamie chided with a grin. "At least I'm pretty, though. I'll give you two some privacy, unless you want a third?"

I looked at Emma, but she hesitated a moment, so I offered her an out. "I'd rather you to myself for now, if that's okay."

She nodded quickly, and I noticed she looked really tired and worn out. As nice as yesterday was—and as much as I wanted to try out new positions with her and explore more of her—she looked like what she could use most of all was a hot bath, a warm bed, and maybe a cuddle partner.

Chapter Seventeen

Emma

I had no idea how I'd gotten this lucky. I'd been really tired from the drinks, and instead of Gauge trying to fuck the exhaustion out of me, he'd drawn me a bath and wasn't even weirdly sexual about it.

He was going to leave me, but I asked him to stay. So he sat with his back against the bathroom wall, fully clothed outside of the tub, and we just talked—about my day, about my life. He wanted to know everything about me.

It was crazy. I never did things like this. I never really felt attraction for other people; now here I was, barging in on a polycule where I felt attraction for two of the three members. I hadn't met their third partner, Rosie, but based on the way Jamie talked about her, I'd be surprised if I wasn't also attracted to her.

I could almost cry from the relief of finally feeling normal and being attracted to real people, not trains. Although, with how many train references Gauge slipped into our conversations, either I've found another person in the world like me, or he had picked up on it and didn't judge me.

I couldn't believe I'd gotten so lucky.

When I got out of the bath, he wrapped me up in a giant warm towel and gave me a comfy button-up shirt of his to wear that fell about halfway down my thigh.

I felt sexy in it, but I was covered unless I bent over or raised my arms up too high.

"Should I be wearing more?"

He just shrugged. "Are you comfortable?"

"Well, yeah, but I don't want to make Rosie uncomfortable."

I already knew Jamie well enough to know this wouldn't bother them at all.

"That's really sweet of you," Gauge said, opening the door to his room and leading me over to the kitchen, "but I doubt there's anything you could do that would make Rosie uncomfortable."

He opened the fridge and was looking at what they had when the door opened. I turned around, not wanting their roommate's first impression of me to be of my ass in Gauge's shirt, but froze where I stood when I saw who'd walked in.

The conductor.

The scorchingly hot conductor from the train the other day.

The one who knee-fucked me in the empty train car.

My jaw dropped. "What?"

She grinned instantly. "Hey gorgeous, you here for me?"

"You know she isn't," Gauge answered for me. It'd been annoying back when Miles used to do that, but it was surprisingly hot when Gauge did it. Probably because he already knew me well enough to anticipate what I was thinking.

"So, you finally made your move," she—*Rosie*—mused with a wicked grin as she prowled toward us. "Good for you."

Jamie walked out into the living room and glanced between me, Gauge and Rosie, before grinning. "Well, everyone's up to speed now, cool."

"Wait, what?" I asked looking at Jamie with alarm.

Jamie bit their lip, saying, "I did it again, didn't I?" They turned to Gauge and asked, "You didn't tell her?"

"About?" he replied.

"That you two knew about the ride I gave Emma the other day?" Rosie filled in.

"So, you're their other partner?" I asked, needing to make sure I understood everything clearly.

"I told her we're poly," Jamie clarified.

"We're all together, if that's what you're asking," Rosie explained. "We like to share."

"Only if you're interested, obviously," Gauge added.

"Obviously," Jamie agreed.

"She is," Rosie answered for me while staring at me with a tilt of her head, daring me to disagree.

"I-I, um..."

Very eloquent. But I was standing in the same room with the only three people I could remember ever being attracted to, all of whom I'd been some level of physical with, and I didn't have the first clue what to say.

"You're coming on too strong," Gauge warned, putting a protective hand on my back.

I shot him a grateful smile before turning back to Rosie. She smirked and replied, "You'll come around, and when you do, Gauge and I can show you and Jamie a good time."

Jamie just rolled their eyes and grabbed Rosie's hand. She looked genuinely surprised when they started to lead her out of the room. Before Jamie closed the door behind both of them, they shot me a wink and mouthed, "You're welcome."

Being here was overwhelming, but in a good way. I was starting to think I was going to like it here.

Chapter Eighteen

Rosie

I was genuinely impressed with Gauge's quick work of getting Emma over here and onboard with our situation.

Today was a day of surprises, though, since Jamie had all but pulled me out of the room to spare Emma and Gauge discomfort. Jamie never took the lead, so them dragging me anywhere was unusual.

They shut the door behind us, and I looked at them questioningly. Instead of speaking, I just waited.

"I like her," they said.

"And you're implying I'd mess it up?"

"I'm implying you're a bit intense. And since she already freaked out a little when I kissed her earlier, we need to be more chill."

"You kissed her?" I asked, half surprised and half jealous I hadn't been there to see it.

Jamie nodded. "Yeah, I thought she knew about Gauge, but he hadn't told her and she got super uncomfortable. I made him tell her, but yeah, we need to cool it."

"By 'we', you mean me?"

"I mean, I wasn't the one who fucked her inside of Gauge, so..."

"You wish you had," I scoffed.

"Maybe a little."

I was startled by their answer. This was a side of them I hadn't seen before.

"What would you do to her?" I asked.

"I didn't do anything—just kissed her."

"But you wouldn't say no to doing more," I pushed. They didn't say anything, so I kept going. "I'm sure the two of you together could put on quite the show for me and Gauge."

"That's the 'too strong' I'm talking about."

"Hard to believe that'd be too strong for her. When I met Emma, she was fucking herself in public on a train."

They shook their head at me. "Still less intense than the orgy you're after."

I raised an eyebrow. "I was with her. She has it in her."

"I don't think she's there yet," Jamie insisted, turning away to listen at the door. "I don't even think she knows about us."

"You just said you guys told her we're together."

"No, no, not that. About what we are."

I paused for a moment. "You don't think he's told her yet?"

"I doubt it. I've been with her most of the day and I really think it would've come up."

"I thought she knew. Isn't she the one fighting to keep our tracks untouched?"

"She is, but she started that before she met any of us."

I sighed, mulling over our predicament. "If they get rid of the tracks, we can't stay—he knows that."

"He probably didn't want to add more to Emma's plate. She's been really stressed out trying to get the island to care about the trains."

She was going to be even more stressed if he left without explaining anything to her. We couldn't stay on the island without the tracks.

I sighed heavily. "He's got to tell her so she knows the stakes. What if we can't stay? He can't be planning to just disappear without telling her."

He was already in deep enough that it would hurt him to leave her. If I was being honest with myself, I was pretty attached to the possibility of her, too. I could see her fitting in quite well with him, me, and Jamie—and not even just sexually. They both already liked her, too.

He had to tell her. There may be some way we could help her, but only if she knew.

"I'm going back out there."

"No," Jamie said quickly. "Give them some time. Maybe he'll come to his senses on his own."

I shook my head. "I'm going out there."

"Please don't."

"What's in it for me?" I asked. We'd played this game enough that they knew exactly what I wanted, the one way to make sure I stayed in the room with them.

They sunk to their knees in front of me, looking up at me and pouting. "Can I please taste you?"

"I don't know," I said, pretending to consider it. "You're being a bit of a brat today. Maybe I should punish you."

"Punish me later if you have to, but don't punish yourself too. Please let me taste you."

I pretended to think about it, but I already knew that even if I was going to spank them later, I was going to indulge them now.

Chapter Nineteen

Emma

I woke up alone, in a strange bed, and it took me a few seconds to realize where I was and why.

I was still at Gauge's apartment. Another few seconds made it obvious why he wasn't lying next to me.

He was standing outside the door, whispering to someone outside. From what I could hear, it sounded like they were arguing.

"I'll tell her eventually. I just need more time."

"We're running out of time," came the heated answer that had to be Rosie.

"We'll figure something out."

"How? We're *trains*! We're not from here, and if she doesn't figure something out, we can't stay."

I was pretty sure I was dreaming now, because none of that made any sense. I must be having a nightmare from all the stress of the Railway project.

"She'll figure it out," Gauge said confidently.

I was glad he was confident about it, because I definitely wasn't.

"If she doesn't, we'll have to leave. Maybe to a different island, maybe leave the planet altogether, but we wouldn't be able to stay."

This was a weird dream. I wondered when I would wake up.

Gauge was quiet, but Rosie continued. "Don't you want to be able to continue riding the rails here? I don't know about you, but I don't want to leave. Especially not now that you found Emma and things are getting interesting."

"I can't leave her," Gauge replied. Everything in me rebelled against his defeated tone.

Before I could think, I answered, "Then don't leave."

They both instantly went quiet and, after a moment, the door slowly opened.

Gauge and Rosie were both standing there, watching me. "How much did you hear?" he asked.

"Nothing that makes sense," I answered honestly, no longer convinced this was a dream.

"So everything then," Rosie said, turning her attention to Gauge and patting him on the back. "Might as well fill in the gaps."

He sighed and came over to the bed, sitting on the end. "So... you might have noticed I'm not exactly like you."

"What do you mean?"

"Well, um, maybe it would be easier to show you," he said, taking the hem of his shirt and pulling it over his head.

What I saw simultaneously made no sense to me yet confirmed I wasn't dreaming. I knew my mind wouldn't be able to manufacture this.

His chest was covered in what looked like tattoos of train tracks. Before I could think better of it, I reached out and touched one of the lines, pulling my hand back quickly in shock at the feel. The tattoos weren't tattoos at all—they were made of metal.

"What are you?" I asked, knowing this wasn't a human abnormality.

"The easiest answer is trains."

"What?"

"You're not explaining it well." Rosie sounded exasperated. "We're not human."

I nodded; it was clear Gauge wasn't human and it wasn't a stretch to believe she wasn't, either. Rosie, Gauge and Jamie all looked otherworldly.

"So, what are you?"

"We're what you would call aliens. We aren't from Earth. Our home planet is made of mostly metal, which is probably why we evolved like we did. But if you want to get more specific, we're metamorphs. We can transform into a secondary form."

"Technically, this is our secondary form," Gauge clarified.

"Unhelpful," Rosie jabbed, rolling her eyes.

"So, what's your primary form?" I asked, trying to follow along.

"Trains," Rosie answered.

I looked between Gauge and Rosie, waiting for someone to tell me this was a cruel joke they were playing on me. They must have figured out I was train-sexual and were having a laugh at me. Except, when I stopped to think about my reality, it started to make more sense and seem more likely that they were being honest.

The fact was, I hadn't felt attraction to anyone in longer than I could remember. Then, for some reason, I was attracted to Gauge, Rosie, and Jamie. For me to be attracted to one of them—never mind all three—was incredibly unlikely. So, what was more likely: that after years of trying to change myself, my sexuality had realigned on its own, or that something inside of me recognized the otherness of them and was attracted to that?

"You're being serious?" I asked, halfway to believing them.

"I know it sounds crazy," he answered.

"It does," I agreed.

"But we can prove it," Rosie said.

"How?" I asked.

"Why don't you take her to see Jamie?"

"Where are they?" I asked.

"They're working, so they'll be running the tracks right now."

"You mean..."

Rosie nodded. "Yes—we're not the conductors. We're the trains."

"If you want to get dressed, I'll bring you to see Jamie," Gauge offered.

I shot out of bed and hurriedly dressed. If they were pranking me, it was an elaborate one, and I wanted to see where they'd go with this. If it was true, I was even more excited.

Chapter Twenty

Emma

Gauge took me into the train's control room, and even though I'd never seen one in person, it looked pretty standard. Nothing out of the ordinary.

Probably the craziest thing I'd seen so far was that apparently they let just anyone walk into the control room.

If they were pulling my leg about being trains, at least they opened my eyes to the new possibilities.

As if reading my mind, Gauge led me to what should have been the conductor's chair and motioned for me to take a seat.

It was pretty clear, though, that no one was here. Unless they had stepped away from their post, the train was driving itself.

The tracks rumbled beneath us, and I felt a rush of heat go straight to my core. The feeling was amplified by the naughtiness of the situation. I wasn't supposed to be in here, this close to the train's center.

The chair seemed to vibrate more around me than it should have, but I tried to focus.

"This doesn't prove anything," I said hesitantly. I felt in my gut that Gauge was telling the truth, but I needed to know for sure.

"Well, I can't morph in front of you since Jamie's already running the track," Gauge explained, "but I can show you that this train is Jamie."

"How?"

"You can text them. It'll come up on the train's console. Here, I'll give you their number."

"That's okay," I said, taking my phone out. "I already have it."

I shot a quick text to Jamie and waited.

Gauge is fucking with me, right?

Gauge was right. It popped up on the train's console. That didn't prove anything, but then a response started to appear.

The train bellowed out, "Choo—Chooo" before a response came through to my phone.

Jamie

Not in the way I want him to be.

The train whistled again and Gauge chuckled. Before I could ask what he was laughing about, another text came through.

I just told him to take you hard against my console.

What do you say, sweetheart?

You want to go for a ride?

I couldn't believe what I was seeing.

If this is really you, tell me what you told me about Rosie

Which thing? I said a lot

The secret thing

"Wooo—Woooo!" whistled the train.

Gauge rolled his eyes. "Fine, fine," he grumbled. Turning to me, he explained. "Jamie told me to close my eyes and insists you don't repeat whatever they say out loud," he said before saying more loudly, "which is incredibly obnoxious because we don't keep secrets from each other and they're just doing this to annoy me."

"Chooo—Choooo!"

"Are too!" Gauge insisted under his breath.

My phone chimed, and I glanced down at Jamie's messages.

He's right I'm just fucking with him

> But I told you Rosie's scared of water

> Full disclosure, G obviously knows that, but it's funny to make him sweat so don't tell him what I said

Just like that, I believed them.

It was *actually* Jamie.

I was riding on a train that was actually an alien who could sometimes look human, with another alien who sometimes looked human, and who both wanted me. And they were train enough that my mind and body both wanted them—badly.

I squirmed a little in the seat, thinking about the possibilities. Of course, another message came in.

> You know I can feel that, right?

"What??"

Gauge's eyes flew open. "What? Is everything okay?"

"You guys can feel things people do on you while you're trains?" I screeched.

His expression turned from concerned to a smirk. "Is that concerning to you?"

"This whole time?" I gasped, feeling mortified.

His silence was answer enough.

"Which one of you was I riding?" I asked slowly, but I already knew the answer.

We were on Jamie now, and Rosie had fucked me on my favorite train.

"Oh my god. You felt it when Rosie fucked me?" I asked Gauge.

He chuckled. "I was too scared to approach you. I didn't think you could ever want someone like me, and she thought I was being crazy and wanted to speed up the process."

"This whole time when I thought I was fucking myself, I was riding you?"

"If you're worried you took advantage of me, it was very welcome," he replied with a smirk,

Standing, I smacked his arm. "That wasn't what I was worried about! I didn't know better! You were watching me!"

Gauge shrugged. "It was hard not to. You were putting on quite a show."

I blushed at that and smacked his arm again. He grabbed my hand and pulled me to him, grabbing my hips and lifting me up onto the console. Onto *Jamie's* console, which started to vibrate under me.

"What are you doing?" I asked.

"Listening to Jamie—unless you want me to stop?" Gauge asked before he started kissing my neck.

"Choooo—Choooo" the train whistled. From the increased vibrations, I assumed Jamie was more than happy with the situation.

"Do you want me to stop?" Gauge asked again. Moving his tongue lower, he licked a trail of kisses to my cleavage. With his lips, the combination of the heat and vibrations of the train—of

Jamie—and knowing how taboo this was, the last thing I wanted was to stop.

"Nooo," I whined.

"No? You want me to stop?" he asked, his hands on the straps of my top, ready to pull them down and expose me at my word.

"No, I want you to keep going."

He yanked one strap down before pausing and asking, "Are you sure?"

I nodded vigorously. "Very."

He pulled my other strap down, exposing my breasts to the cool air for a moment before his mouth was on one and his hand on the other.

I moaned at the contact as he worked my nipples.

"Woooo—Wooooo!"

Apparently, Jamie was enjoying this too.

When he pulled away, Gauge murmured, "You want to get Jamie really worked up?"

"What are you thinking?" I asked, knowing already that I'd say yes.

"Jamie, can you disable the brake lever?"

"Choo—Chooo," the train sounded excitedly.

I looked around, wondering what Gauge was planning, when I saw what he had to be talking about. There were different buttons, levers and controls on the control panel but there was a long, thick lever that stood pretty close to the length and girth of Gauge's cock.

He winked at me as he pulled the lever from its upright position, moving it toward him until it was angled diagonally.

"What do you say you take Jamie for a ride?" he asked, motioning to the lever.

I felt like my body was on fire and so badly wanted something inside of me, but Jamie's lever was thick.

"I don't know if it'll fit..." I said uneasily.

"Woo—Wooo!"

Gauge chuckled. "You're going to give Jamie an ego. They're not any bigger than I am."

"Choo—Choo!" Jamie managed to make the whistle sound offended.

Gauge just laughed and picked me up, moving me over and positioning me on all fours around the lever. I felt it pressing against my entrance, pulsing.

"What about you?" I asked.

"I'll watch you get settled, and then see what that pretty mouth of yours can do."

If I wasn't already dripping, that would've done it.

I pushed myself back onto the lever slowly, getting used to the feel.

"Why don't you whip it out and show me what I'm working toward?" I cooed.

He grinned, saying, "I normally don't take orders, but you asked so nicely."

I sunk further down onto the lever. I must've been about halfway and was already feeling full.

Gauge started to stroke his already erect shaft. I pushed myself down further, letting out a loud moan that was greeted with an encouraging, "Wooo—Woooo!"

"Almost there," Gauge groaned. "Better hurry up, though. Wouldn't want to get to our destination without us getting off first."

It wouldn't take me long once I was completely full, but he was right. I was impatient to be filled by both of them.

I pushed myself back a little more and was relieved when I sunk all the way to the console.

I opened my mouth expectantly and was rewarded with Gauge's grin as he stepped forward, using his hand to direct his shaft to my waiting mouth.

"Go easy on her, Jam," he instructed as he pressed himself into my mouth.

"Woooo—Woooooo," Jamie whistled as the lever inside me began to pulse harder.

I moaned loudly as Gauge continued to push his length down my throat.

I wasn't going to last long being stretched at both ends.

Just as I was thinking that, Gauge told me to grab onto the edge of the console. I did immediately.

"What a good little rail slut," he growled as he grabbed onto my hips, pulled me forward before pushing me back hard onto the lever. He continued to move me, fucking me against Jamie. I moaned around his cock in my mouth as the tension built up inside me.

Gauge groaned and locked his gaze with mine. "What do you say, Em? Are you ready to come with me?"

I moaned in answer and he thrust me a bit harder, saying, "So close, let's get there together." With one more thrust, I was falling over the edge.

There was a loud whistle from both the train and from Gauge. Then my mouth flooded with a tasteless steam that had me fighting to breathe. Gauge pulled out quickly before the steam could completely overwhelm me.

With my mouth now free, I started to cough.

He pulled me into a hug, rubbing my back as I coughed. "You're okay. You were so good for us," he murmured.

"Wooo—Woooo," Jamie agreed.

When I stopped coughing, Gauge slowly lifted me off the lever, pulling me into his lap on the conductor's chair. I snuggled against him, feeling like I was home for the first time in a long time.

"So... what do you think?" Gauge asked.

"Huh?" I asked, somewhat sleepily.

"Do you believe me now?"

"Yes." I couldn't doubt it anymore.

"And did you like it?"

I blushed at that, knowing he already knew I did.

He chuckled. "I'll amend that. Did you like it enough that you could get used to it?"

"I don't know if I'll ever get used to that," I answered honestly. It was the most mind-blowing sex I'd ever had. There was likely no getting used to that. Especially if, or rather *when*, we introduced

Rosie into the mix. I knew from experience how fiery she was and couldn't wait to see what she would have planned for everyone in the bedroom.

"I don't think you'll ever get me used to it, but I'd sure like to see you try," I told him.

He grinned. "You're perfect. I told them we got damn lucky with you."

"I'm the lucky one."

"We can all count ourselves lucky once we solve the train issue," he said.

I snuggled closer to him. "What will happen if the tracks are destroyed? Will you be okay?"

"We'll be alright, but we'd have to leave. That's the last thing any of us want to do."

I furrowed my brow. "You won't have to. We'll fix things, some-how."

"If anyone can, it's you," Gauge insisted as he lifted my straps and put my shirt back into place. "I believe in you. Let's get you home so you can rest and we can come up with a plan."

When we got back to their apartment, his bed greeted me and dragged me almost immediately into sleep.

Chapter Twenty-One

Emma

When I woke up, Gauge was lying in bed with me. He pulled me tighter into him and asked, "Were you dreaming about me?"

"I don't really remember. Why?"

"You were mumbling something about a train, and since I'm obviously your favorite train—"

"For now!" Jamie's voice boomed through the open door.

I rolled my eyes and smirked. "If you guys are listening already, you might as well come in."

"Like I need permission," Rosie said, pushing the door the rest of the way open with Jamie close on her heels.

She took the armchair in the corner of the room and sat down, facing the bed.

Jamie hopped on the bed and crawled over to me. "Good to see you again, sweetheart."

I blushed a little at that, but they didn't give me a chance to feel weird about it. Instead, they wrapped their leg over mine, trapping me between them and Gauge, and kissed me.

I felt Gauge's hum of approval on my back as I lost myself to Jamie's kiss.

"I thought we were trying to plan." Rosie's voice snapped me out of the moment.

I pulled back from Jamie, who turned their attention to Rosie and asked, "Really?"

"Really. Didn't I tell you that you had to behave?"

I was surprised that Jamie listened to her and didn't move to kiss me again. Instead, they nuzzled into my neck, grumbling, "Fine. But I'm staying here."

"As long as you don't distract us. I actually had an idea," Rosie said. "You work for the tourism board, right?"

I nodded, surprised she knew that.

"Well, Gauge said you've been focusing your efforts on the locals. But what if we get the tourists excited about the trains?"

"Like, play up their history on the island?" I asked, thinking through the idea.

There was some precedent for that, with many of the buildings on the island being protected by the historical preservation committee. If I could find evidence of their importance, it might be enough to work.

"I meant local tours, but whatever works."

"And we could do theme nights!" Jamie added with enough excitement that I had to laugh.

"What kind of themes?"

"Seasonal themes, holiday themes. We could even do a historical themed tour if you think that would work."

I mulled over the thought for a moment. "If we did tours, I could tie it into my job. I could get paid to play conductor."

"I'd let you be my conductor any day," Jamie teased, making me laugh.

"But more importantly," I continued, "if I'm able to find a historical significance to the rails, the town hall would have to put a stop to the demolition. Rosie, you're brilliant!"

She shrugged. "That's not normally what people call me, but thank you."

"Don't let her take all the credit," Gauge argued. "It was mostly your idea."

"Anyone up for a trip to the library?" I asked, looking around.

"I'll stay, I'm just the idea woman," Rosie replied with a wink. I laughed at that and wasn't surprised in the slightest when Jamie agreed, saying "I'll stay too. Someone's got to keep her company. Besides, I'd be a distraction. We'll stay and let you actually get some work done."

"I'm going," Gauge said.

"Just don't go distracting our girl," Jamie demanded, making me flush a little, but I definitely didn't mind being called that.

"She'll find what we need and then we can come back here and all celebrate," Gauge beamed. I loved his confidence in me and loved the idea of a group celebration even more.

Chapter Twenty-Two

Gauge

It took all of my very limited self-control to let Emma peruse the library shelves unmolested, but I knew how important this was and was as eager as she was to get the hard part over with so we could get to celebrating.

We were browsing the local history section, and while she was looking at the book titles, I couldn't stop watching her.

I knew I wasn't being helpful, but at least I wasn't hindering her process, so I counted it as a win.

She eventually pulled out a few books and handed them to me. I grabbed them and waited while she continued to pile more into my arms. When I couldn't see her over the stack I was holding, she finally said, "Okay, that's probably good enough."

"You think?" I asked, raising an amused eyebrow at her. "How long do you plan to be here?"

"As long as it takes."

I would have been worried if I wasn't sure the librarian would kick us out at some point.

A few hours in and my eyes were swimming from all the reading I'd done. I hadn't found anything helpful and was grateful when the librarian started to make her rounds, knowing we'd be kicked out and could stop reading for tonight.

Except when the librarian got to us, she saw Emma and smiled. "Long night?" she asked.

"It will be if I have anything to say about it," Emma replied. "It's for the Save the Railways project."

The librarian nodded. "Stay as long as you like. You know you have my support, and please let me know if there's anything I can do to help."

I fought not to groan at the fact that we might be here all night. Thankfully, Emma was too distracted to catch my disappointment, and told the librarian, "Actually, there might be something you can do. I'm trying to find something—anything really, grasping at straws over here—that proves the railways should be considered a historical landmark—"

"Which would lend them historical protection and stop the motorway initiative in its tracks. That's brilliant!" the librarian added.

Emma nodded enthusiastically. "If I can pull it off. So far, I haven't found anything useful. Any recommendations?"

The librarian looked thoughtfully at the books in front of us. After a moment, she pulled a title from my pile, asking Emma, "Have you read this one yet?"

"Not yet," she replied, taking it from the librarian's hands and opening it to the table of contents. "What are we looking for?"

"If I'm remembering right, you'll want the section on the flood of '94."

Emma ran her finger down the index, found what she was looking for, and quickly flipped to the page. Her eyes lit up when she saw the headline.

"This might work!" she said. "Thank you!"

"Thank me if it works out. If not, we'll keep trying," the librarian said. "Us locals have to stick together. Stick it to the man."

Emma laughed, but her attention was mostly focused on the book, so the librarian excused herself to make the rest of her rounds.

A few minutes later, she looked up at me with a grin. "We've got it."

"It'll work?"

"Absolutely. Miles and the rest of Big Car-ma are going down."

I grinned at the look on Emma's face. "You look like you'll eat him alive. It shouldn't turn me on, but *engines*, it's hot."

"We'll destroy them. I just need to take some copies of this, and then we can go home."

"To celebrate."

"Definitely," she said with a smile that was colored by her blush.

Chapter Twenty-Three

Rosie

The door burst open to an excited Emma, with Gauge following closely behind.

"Found something good?" I asked.

"Of course she did, she's a genius," Gauge answered, making a delicious blush spread across Emma's face.

"I knew you could do it," Jamie told her from the kitchen where they were already pouring champagne for us.

"You guys had more faith in me than I did," she admitted.

"We were so confident, Jamie's already pouring the victory champagne for our little celebration," I told her.

She smiled at that, bouncing over to the kitchen to help Jamie. Gauge came over to me and I asked quietly, "Will it work?"

I knew Gauge well enough to know he'd be acting this excited just to keep Emma's spirits up even if he wasn't as hopeful.

He nodded. "I think so. The odds are pretty good, anyway."

"Good enough for me," I replied quietly before raising my voice. "Jamie, why don't you take off your shirt and get over here?"

I knew Emma was a little nervous. I figured that if I focused on Jamie, it would help her calm down.

"Where do you want me?" Jamie asked, already shirtless and in front of me.

I looked over at Gauge, making it clear he was my partner in this. Gauge and I loved tag-teaming Jamie. Adding Emma into the mix was going to make this a lot more interesting.

"My room," he said after a minute. "There'll be room for everyone on the bed."

Jamie winked at Emma, calling out, "Race you there!"

I was surprised when she grinned and started sprinting toward the bedroom. The two of them got there at pretty much the same time, but Jamie fell back, letting her win.

They were really both so adorable. I couldn't wait to make them moan all night.

Gauge and I looked at each other and laughed before following them to the bedroom.

Chapter Twenty-Four

Emma

I was a little nervous, which was ridiculous since I'd been with all of them already. Together seemed like it might be a lot, but I was pretty sure I was going to love it.

I knew they'd take good care of me; a feeling which was only emphasized when Gauge leaned in and whispered that we'd take it slow and told me I could stop any time I wanted.

I didn't want to, though.

I let him lead me to the bed with his lips on mine as he stripped me out of my shirt. He laid me down and started kissing me every-where. My moans were joined with whistles of pleasure from the other side of the bed.

Gauge took my hands from his chest and moved them over my head, where they brushed against Jamie's. I went to move my hands, but Jamie grasped them with their hands, squeezing them gently in time to their moans.

The closest Gauge had gotten to my center was dragging my pants and panties off, but I was already drenched. The idea that Rosie was watching us and devouring Jamie the same way Gauge was devouring me was too hot for me to not be soaked and ready.

"Turn over," Rosie ordered, and I felt Jamie squeeze my hands gently before releasing them and following her request.

Gauge brought his lips to my ear and said, "Up and on all fours."

Surprised and excited, I rushed to comply. The position put me eye to eye with Jamie, who was grinning at me. Rosie was standing next to the bed behind them wearing a strap-on.

"Normally they're fighting over me, so it's good to have someone to share the attention with," Jamie told me.

"You're really an insufferable little thing," Rosie said, smacking Jamie on the ass.

They jumped a little at the contact, taunting, "You'll have to find a way to shut me up."

"Emma, stick your tongue in Jamie's mouth and get us some peace and quiet," Rosie groaned.

"Yes, please!" Jamie grinned.

I didn't need more of an invitation. I crossed the small distance between us and put my lips on theirs before dipping my tongue inside their mouth.

The moment I did, I felt Gauge slap my ass. I let out a little yelp which faded into a moan when he pushed himself inside me.

From Jamie's reaction, I was pretty sure Rosie was doing the same to them.

We were pressed together hard as Rosie and Gauge thrust in and out of us, and I lost myself to the pleasure. Mine and Jamie's tongues mingled with my moans and their whistles.

The pressure ramped up and up until I felt like I was going to burst, only for Gauge to stop.

I pulled away from Jamie and whined, "Please don't stop."

Gauge grinned wickedly. "Rosie wanted the honors of your first orgasm of the night. Switch places and ask nicely, and I'm sure she'll get you there."

I'd been a little nervous before, but now I was too far gone to care. I crawled past Jamie, right up to Rosie's strap-on and took it deep down my throat.

"Woah there, someone's eager," she teased.

I sucked the silicone for a minute before she pulled back and said, "Since you asked so nicely, turn around."

I did immediately, causing her to laugh. Jamie and Gauge were both watching me with hunger in their eyes as I moved to where Jamie had been.

"Jamie, lips to yourself this time. I want to hear her begging."

This time, Jamie moved their hands to mine and interlaced our fingers.

"Bet you I can get there faster than you," Jamie said with a wink.

It wasn't even going to be a competition. I was still right on the edge, and I hated to lose.

"You're onnnnnnn." It came out like a moan as Rosie pushed into me.

A few strokes later and I came loudly, not bothering to quiet my moans. Rosie had said she wanted to hear me, so I let probably the whole island hear as well.

"That's my girl," Gauge growled while still pounding into Jamie.

"Our girl," Rosie corrected, squeezing my ass playfully while I lay there recovering.

A moment later, Jamie came with a "Woooo—wooooo," rivaling my loudest moan before they collapsed on the bed next to me, pulling me onto their chest and cuddling me up with them.

We went one more round that night before I was too exhausted to move, and Gauge insisted we call it a night.

Jamie and Rosie didn't bother to leave. The bed was big enough to comfortably fit all of us. I fell asleep laying on Jamie's chest with Gauge pressed against my back.

I could get used to this.

Chapter Twenty-Five

Emma

Seeing the look on Miles's face as I waltzed into the town hall meeting on the arms of Gauge and Jamie, with Rosie flanking us in her conductor's outfit, was only narrowly beaten by the look in his eyes when he realized I'd won.

He left the meeting abruptly, arguing into his phone. He'd called Daddy asking him to fix things, but there wasn't anything he could do.

The trains held historical significance to the island. Years ago, the trains had saved hundreds of lives by moving people quickly away from floodwater on one side of the island. The cars hadn't been able to function in the water, and if it hadn't been for the trains running hundreds of people to safety as quickly as they did, many lives would have been lost.

Of course, it wasn't my trains all those years ago, but that didn't matter. The historical preservation committee agreed that the tracks, and by extension any train running them, were protected.

I'd shown Miles that he couldn't mess with me, my trains, or my island again and I was sure he'd be leaving soon.

The only thing better than the devastation on Miles's face was the feeling of being worshipped by Gauge, Rosie and Jamie later that night.

I saved them from having to leave their home, and they all lavished me in appreciation.

My island was their home, but it was becoming incredibly clear that they were mine.

Epilogue

Emma

"And that's where the flood waters overwhelmed the cars," I told the oohhing and ahhhing tourists.

The tours had been a big enough success that my boss let me out of the office to run them most days. They were a little gimmicky, but they attracted more tourists than we'd seen in a long time.

Jamie also ran some of the tours and was a crowd favorite. They were a born performer and really got into the role.

Today I was giving the tour on Gauge's train, and I couldn't wait for my break.

I'd moved in with Gauge, Rosie and Jamie, and certainly couldn't complain about any lack of attention, but I was dying to take a ride on Gauge today.

I was already thinking about how, on my break, I would slip into the control room and ride him until the whole island could hear his whistles.

I'm sure the island was starting to get used to it though, since the confusion about the midnight train whistles had quickly died down. This was good for me, since I certainly wasn't going to stop riding the rails at all hours of the night.

My trains certainly were reliable in getting me to my destination every night, usually multiple times a night.

I pointed out the last point of interest on the tour and hear a "Choo—Chooo." I'd gotten somewhat better at understanding their meaning. This one was easy, though—Gauge was as impatient as I was.

I laughed a little under my breath, saying, "That's all for now, folks. Please enjoy the rest of your ride. I have to go check in on the train, but I'll be back out before our journey finishes."

And after I do, I thought to myself with a little chuckle, before slipping away and into the control room.

It was wild to me that just a few months ago, I would've given anything to be a normal girl with a normal sexuality. Now, I couldn't believe how foolish I'd been. Everything good about my life now—the island, my job, and my trains—was because I was train-sexual, and I wouldn't change a thing about it.

Your Conductor

Zane E Stori (she/her) is a chaos bisexual who lives for a good pun. Zane has never met a bit she wouldn't commit to. Her entire goal as an author is to make you tilt your head in confusion and ask yourself and others why these books exist. Packed full of puns and queer joy, Zane hopes her stories bring a little bit of humor and queer joy back into the world.

Zane E. Stori is the (maybe still) secret pen name of another queer author who very much didn't want her elderly grandmother reading about train sex. Fun fact: the name Zane E. Stori shares 6 letters with the author's other name.

You can find Zane E. Stori on Instagram @AuthorZaneEStori.

Zane has no idea where the future of their stories are going, but their DMs are always open for pun-related writing suggestions, and if the suggestion hits just right, maybe the next book will be dedicated to you.

Acknowledgments

This story shouldn't have existed. There are so many people that could have stopped this and chose, for better or worse, to encourage me. You can decide whether or not that's a good thing.

Thank you to HR, LR, and RE who sparked this idea in me at a late night hotel party – even though none of you (to my knowledge) wrote your own wacky ideas, you were there for me every step of the way encouraging me and without you all this book definitely wouldn't exist, love you all.

Thank you to Vera Valentine who encouraged me to write this when I was struggling with whether it would find its readers, you're amazing!

Thank you to Steph and Jules who, despite being surprised by the subject of the story, were super down to support it and me.

Thank you to my Book Club Besties who were immediately in at train shifters – we're a weird bunch and I love you all.

Thank you to my editor Kendra and my audiobook narrator Cass for working on this crazy ride with me.

Thank you to Sarah (aka my biggest hater and/or supporter depending on the day) who definitely kept this book alive when it otherwise might not have been written. You're the best.

And to everyone who picked up this book after seeing "train shifters" and needed to know more, I hope this was what you wanted and that you aren't able to look at trains the same way again.

You're Welcome.